The Blue Beyond

For Poppy and Violet, with love x
— Jeanne

For Tabby, with love
— Bethany

STRIPES PUBLISHING LIMITED
An imprint of the Little Tiger Group
1 Coda Studios, 189 Munster Road, London SW6 6AW

First published in Great Britain in 2020

Text copyright © Jeanne Willis, 2020
Illustrations © Bethany Christou, 2020

ISBN: 978-1-78895-173-9

The right of Jeanne Willis and Bethany Christou to be identified as
the author and illustrator of this work respectively has been asserted
by them in accordance with the Copyright, Designs and Patents Act, 1988.

STP/1800/0301/0220

Printed and bound in China.

The Forest Stewardship Council® (FSC®) is a global, not-for-profit organization dedicated to
the promotion of responsible forest management worldwide. FSC defines standards based on
agreed principles for responsible forest stewardship that are supported by environmental, social,
and economic stakeholders. To learn more, visit www.fsc.org

2 4 6 8 10 9 7 5 3 1

The Blue Beyond

Jeanne Willis & Bethany Christou

LITTLE TIGER
LONDON

It was dawn, and as the sun rose above the sleepy lagoon, Lana the butterflyfish rocked gently in her seaweed cradle, blowing bubbles in her dreams. They were little bubbles because she was only a little fish, but her dreams were big – far bigger than she was. She wanted to be the greatest explorer in the world!

As far as Lana knew, the lagoon *was* the whole world. Every day, she woke up in the same safe water with the same best friends and played her same favourite game. And today was no different. "Let's play Explorers!" she called as she swam over to her friends.

The other butterflyfish formed a shoal and followed as Lana darted about, searching for new places, new faces, new *anything*. The fact that everything was exactly the same as yesterday didn't matter – if she couldn't find anything new, she just used her imagination.

"Wow! I've found a mermaid's comb!" Lana called.

The shoal shimmied over and gazed at the long, spikey shell sticking out of the sand. "Wow!" they echoed.

"Let's look for mermaids... Follow me!" said Lana.

Lana and her friends spent a wonderful day looking for mermaids. They didn't find any but nobody minded because Lana thought they might find one tomorrow.

"Meet me in the morning," she instructed, before making her way home.

As Lana drifted off to sleep that night she dreamed she heard the salty sea song of a humpback whale and although she had never met a whale before, she understood every word.

"Swim away, little fish, on the foaming tide,

There's a big brave world on the other side,

Where the dolphins ride on the ocean wide,

Swim away, swim away, swim away."

7

When Lana woke, she couldn't get the song out of her head. Was there really a big brave world out there? What a wonderful place it would be to have a great adventure!

I have to go and find out if the whale is telling the truth! she thought. She went to tell her friends who were waiting to look for mermaids.

"There's been a change of plan," said Lana. She repeated what the dream whale had told her about the world beyond the reef.

They listened with open mouths. "Is it true?"

"If I want to be a great explorer, I must follow my dream and find out," she replied.

There was only one problem — how? The coral reef that circled the lagoon was too high to swim over and there were no waves to carry her. Lana fanned her fins and thrashed her tail to try and make a wave, but all she could manage was a soft ripple.

"If only I was bigger! If only I had more fins! If only I had more tails!" she grumbled.

"You have us!" called her friends.

"That's it!" Lana beamed. "Between us, we have hundreds of fins and tails. Together we can make big waves. Altogether now – one, two, three!"

All the butterflyfish flapped their fins and thrashed their tails until the water began to froth, roll, crash and splash. It formed a giant wave that carried Lara higher and higher, right over the top of the reef. "Woo-hoo! This will be the best adventure ever!" Lana exclaimed.

The shoal listened for a little splash
to make sure that she had landed.
"Stay safe!" they called as the lagoon
returned to its calm, quiet self.

But on the other side of the reef, the
waves were wild. Lana gazed at the
never-ending sea of blue – the dream
whale had told the truth.

At first, Lana felt bold and brave but as the tide tugged her further out to sea, she began to feel anxious and lonely.

"I wish I had someone to share my adventure with." She sighed.

Then beneath the waves, a shadow appeared, gliding silently along. She wasn't alone! Lana had no idea what it was so she froze. But with a loud snort, a scaly snout poked out of the water, followed by a pair of wise, brown eyes.

"Ahoy there!" said the friendly sea turtle.
"What's a little fish like you doing in the
wide open sea?"

"I'm having a big adventure!" exclaimed
Lana.

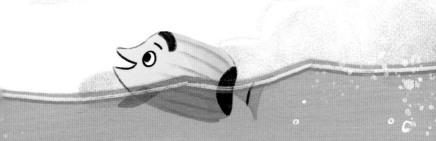

"You've come to the right place." Turtle beamed. "I've lived in this ocean for a hundred years and seen creatures beyond your wildest imagination!"

"The dream whale told me about them," said Lana.

The turtle patted her gently with a leathery flipper. "Did he now?" she asked. "A dream ocean is one thing, but this is a *real* one — which is a very different kettle of fish. There are things that sting and sharks with jagged teeth."

"That won't stop me. I want to be the greatest explorer in the world!" Lana insisted.

"You're a brave fish," Turtle replied. "But while the sea is beautiful, it can also be dangerous. It would be foolish to travel alone."

"Come with me then!" said Lana. "If you can keep up, Grandma." And she blew a raspberry! Turtle pretended to be shocked, then threw back her head and laughed.

"I may be old but I know this ocean like the back of my flipper. Besides, it would be nice to have someone to talk to."

Lana wiggled with excitement and, shielded by the turtle's enormous shell, she dived down to explore the seabed.

"Can you see Ray?" said Turtle. "He has both eyes on one side of his face."

"Where?" asked Lana.

"There in the sand!" replied Turtle, waving a flipper. "He's a master of disguise."

Lana poked about and suddenly a flat fish who was the same colour as the sand shot back in surprise and flapped away like a startled pancake.

"Come back!" called Lana. "I just want to play!"

Then a funny creature came chugging along. "That's a sea cucumber!" Turtle whispered.

As it shuffled away, Lana noticed a tiny face poking out of its behind.

"It's got something sticking out of its bottom!" she announced.

"It's a pearlfish," explained Turtle. "And that's where it likes to live. Don't ask me why, strange things happen at sea!"

Strange, but nothing to be afraid of, thought Lana, and filled with new confidence, she swam off to play with an octopus.

"Hi, Mr Eight Arms!" she said, holding out her fin and shaking each arm in turn.

Delighted with his new friend, Octopus whirled her round and round. "Whee! Faster!" shrieked Lana.

"Stop whirling, please, Octopus!" Turtle scolded playfully. "You'll make her dizzy."

Octopus put Lana down and as he zig-zagged away, he squirted Turtle with a jet of black ink. It was the silliest thing Lana had ever seen — even Turtle could see the funny side.

"I asked for that, stopping his game!" Turtle laughed. "Lana? Where have you gone?" To her horror, Lana was jumping up and down on a plump jellyfish.

"We're playing Bouncy Castles!" she whooped.

"Boing! Boing! Boing!"

"I do apologize, Jellyfish," said Turtle. "Lana is just learning her sea-manners, so *please* don't sting her. She's a friend of mine."

"I won't," promised Jellyfish. "I'm enjoying myself enormously. I was feeling old and invisible but playing with Lana has given me my bounce back. You should try it!"

"OK!" agreed Turtle and, to Jellyfish's shock, she jumped up and down on her.

"I meant try playing with Lana, not try bouncing!" she complained, tossing Turtle on to her shell.

"Oops, sorry!" Turtle apologized, rocking clumsily until she was the right way up. "Come along, Lana. I think Jellyfish is right – I should play with you!"

"Can we play Grandmother's Footsteps?" asked Lana. "You have to creep up on a shellfish and touch it while its shell's shut."

"Well, I *am* a grandmother," said Turtle. "And I can creep. Let's play!"

Lana swam off eagerly to find a suitable shellfish. "I'll go first!" she called.

The shellfish was closed and, thinking it was asleep, Lana began to sneak up. As she did, the shell opened a crack and Lana stopped still. As soon as it closed again, she crept closer. The shell opened wider. Lana stopped, waited for it to close, then swam as fast as she could towards it and touched it as it sprang wide open.

"I did it!" yelled Lana, hovering just inside the shell.

"Look out!" shrieked Turtle. "It's a giant clam! They trap fish!"

Turtle stuck the tip of her flipper inside the clam's shell, letting Lana slip through the gap. Annoyed, the clam slammed shut.

"Oof! Ow..." Turtle yanked her flipper away.

"Oh no! Does it hurt?" asked Lana.

"Just chipped a claw," tutted Turtle. "It'll grow back."

"Your turn to play!" Lana sang.

"Let's play I-Spy instead," Turtle suggested. "No one ever got into trouble playing I-Spy."

"We play that in the lagoon but it's too easy," said Lana. "My shoal always spy something beginning with B."

But Turtle wasn't listening. She was swimming towards the surface.

"The answer is always B for Butterflyfish…"
Lana tailed off, hurrying after Turtle. "Where
are we going? What have you seen?"

Just then, she heard loud squeals, whistles and clicks.

"I spy something beginning with D!" called Turtle.

"Hmmm... Dragonfish?" Lana guessed.

She swam after Turtle into the sunlight,
and there she saw the sight she had
dreamed of...

"D for dolphins!" Lana cried, watching the
dolphins leap and splash, their shiny bodies
making arches in the waves.

"I'd love to ride on one!" said Lana. As the first dolphin passed by, it flicked her on to its back and looped off through the waves.

"Wait for me!" yelled Turtle, puffing after them. By the time she'd caught up, she was exhausted.

"Jump on!" called Lana. "It's the best fun!"

"I think … I'll … sit this one out," wheezed Turtle.

By the time Lana returned, Turtle was snoring on a rock. This amused the dolphin and before it sped away, it squirted water in her face to wake her up.

"Storm at sea!" Turtle spluttered, still half asleep.

"It was just the dolphin!" giggled Lana. "There's no storm. It's a lovely calm day."

Turtle blinked at her slowly. "Not from where
I'm sitting!" she said. "I've been squirted,
bounced and clipped by a clam. Would you
mind if we did something quiet for a while?"

"Can it involve exploring?" Lana replied.

"We could visit the seahorses," suggested Turtle.

Lana's eyes opened wide in amazement.

"Do they really exist?" she asked.

"You'll see … then you won't … then you will!" replied Turtle mysteriously.

She dragged herself awkwardly to the edge of the rock. But once she had slipped back into the sea, she was her old self again, gliding effortlessly like a bird flying in a windless sky with Lana by her side.

When they arrived, the seahorses were drifting in a pasture of seagrass like ghostly miniature ponies. "Hello!" called Lana.

"Shhh," whispered Turtle. "They're very shy." But it was too late. The seahorses had vanished!

"Where did they go?" wondered Lana, looking all around.

"Nowhere," Turtle murmured. "If you startle them, they change colour to blend in with their surroundings. Watch quietly, keep still and you'll see them." Sure enough, the seahorses turned from green to orange again and reappeared in exactly the same place, as if by magic!

"They must be brilliant at hide and seek!"
said Lana. "That's what we should play!
Shut your eyes, count to one hundred and
I'll go and hide."

"All right, but don't go too far! One,"
counted Turtle. "Two...!"

"No peeking!" called Lana as she swam off to look for a good hiding place. Where could she hide… In a cave? Inside a sea anemone? Under the wings of a dozing ray? No, Turtle would find her straight away! Desperate to win the game, Lana swam further and further — without looking where she was going.

When she finally stopped, she realized she had no idea where she was. "Turtle?" she called, darting back and forth. "Turtle?"

There was no reply. Lana spun round, looking anxiously for the rocks she'd swum past earlier, hoping they would lead her back, but they had disappeared.

Suddenly the ocean felt cold and eerie and Lana began to wish she was safely in the lagoon with her shoal. She waited and waited for Turtle to come but there was no sign of her. Lana started to panic.

"I'm lost!" she cried. "Help! Help!"

The sea began to stir and to her surprise,
her cry was answered.

"All by yourself, little one?" hissed a
slippery voice. "Lost, are you? That *is* a
crying shame."

She watched as a triangular fin circled closer. "Who are you?" asked Lana.

"I'm your new best friend," replied the voice.

"I've made a lot of new friends today!" said Lana proudly.

"Really?" smirked the voice. "If they were *real* friends they'd be here, wouldn't they?"

Lana wasn't sure what to think. "I have old friends," she insisted. "A whole shoal of them! I should get back..."

"Oh, *those* friends," laughed whoever it was. "I know where they are. Come with me."

Lana couldn't believe her luck! As the shadow turned with a flick of its forked tail she followed it, but to her dismay it was taking her further out to sea.

"Is this definitely the right way?" she asked.

"Nearly there," the voice told her as they dived deeper.

At the bottom of the sea there was an old shipwreck covered in barnacles.

"In you go," said her new friend,
giving Lana a shove.

"My old friends don't live there!" she cried.

"No, but I do!" the voice
declared. By the light of a
glowing anglerfish, Lana
saw its jagged teeth and,
trembling, she remembered
what Turtle had told her
about real oceans.

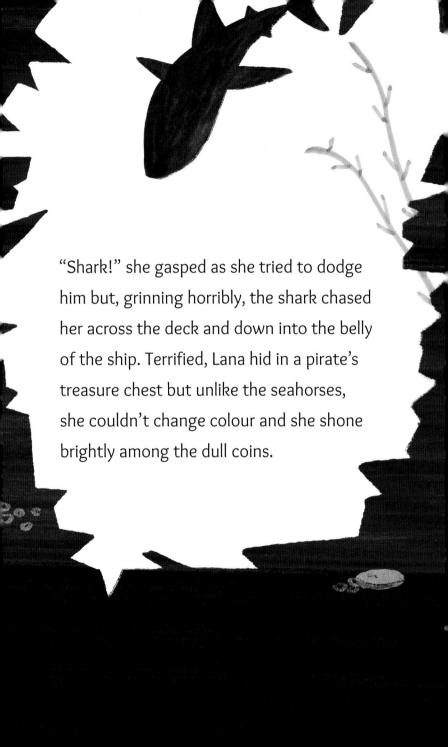

"Shark!" she gasped as she tried to dodge him but, grinning horribly, the shark chased her across the deck and down into the belly of the ship. Terrified, Lana hid in a pirate's treasure chest but unlike the seahorses, she couldn't change colour and she shone brightly among the dull coins.

"I'm coming to get you!" said Shark, snapping his jaws. He was about to eat her when something grabbed his tail with its razor-sharp beak and dragged him backwards.

"No! I'm coming to get *you!*" shouted Turtle. "Give me a hand, Octopus!"

"I'll give you eight!" said Octopus, grabbing Shark and spinning him round.

Just then Jellyfish arrived, waving her
tentacles furiously at Shark.
"Be off or I'll sting you!"

Shark twisted and turned. He was about to sink his teeth into Turtle's tail when Lana heard loud clicks and whistles. It was the dolphins! Seeing Lana and her friends in danger, they cornered Shark and chased him back out to sea.

"That taught him — never mess with my friends!" announced Turtle, blowing a raspberry.

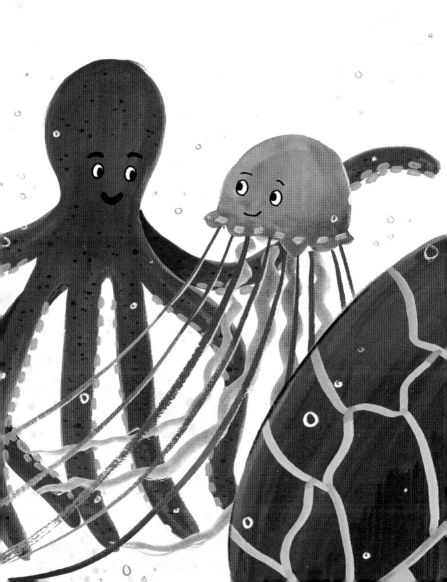

"*I* taught *you* that!" laughed Lana. "Thank you for saving me, everyone."

"You're welcome," said Turtle. "We didn't want your first adventure to be your last."

The sun was setting. "Goodness, is it that late already?" Turtle noted. "Time flies when you're having fun, doesn't it?"

"I've had such an exciting day," said Lana, with a little yawn.

"Me too," replied Turtle. "But it's nearly bedtime. Shall I take you home?"

"Yes, please," said Lana. "My friends will be waiting to hear about my adventure! But how will I get back over the reef?"

Turtle put a flipper round her. "Don't worry," she reassured Lana. "I've saved the best until last..."

Lana swam beside her with Octopus and Jellyfish until she saw the reef in the distance. Turtle held up a flipper. "Stop!" she commanded.

"Why, are you tired?" asked Lana.

"I'm as fresh as a kipper," insisted Turtle.
"It's all part of my plan. Listen…"

Lana listened, and over the roar of the waves
she heard a familiar salty sea song.

"Go home, little fish, go home to bed,

Float by the blowhole on my head,

And I will squirt you back instead,

Fly home, little fish, fly home!"

It was the humpback whale!

"Am I dreaming?" asked Lana.

"No!" Turtle laughed. "He's definitely real."

The whale swam towards Lana with the widest smile she'd ever seen. Turtle guided her over his blowhole.

"That was the best adventure ever!" said Lana. "Thank you for making my dream come true, Turtle."

"You did that all by yourself." Turtle smiled. "Never stop dreaming!"

As Octopus waved farewell and Jellyfish wiped away a tear, the whale blasted a great fountain of water out of his blowhole. It carried Lana up to the stars and dropped her with a soft splash back into the lagoon.

"Goodbye, Greatest Little Explorer," murmured Turtle. "Sweet dreams!"

"Hooray! Lana's home!" chorused the shoal of butterflyfish. "Did you find a mermaid?"

"I met a friendly turtle and a scary shark," said Lana as they gathered round her. "And a sea cucumber who had a pearl fish up his—"

"Tell us everything!" the shoal interrupted.

So Lana told them all about her great adventure long into the night. When she finally fell asleep in her seaweed cradle, she heard the song of the dream whale for the last time.

"Brave little fish, you had such fun,

Your daring-do has all been done,

Greatest explorer under the sun!

Go to sleep, little fish. Go ... to ... sleep."

As she slept, Lana heard Turtle calling, "Come and see me soon! There's so much more to explore..." and she dreamed of the amazing adventures she was going to have.

The End